Folktales fro CHINA

MW01616679

retold by Barbara Lawson
illustrated by Kristina Swarner

Table of Contents

SCHOLASTIC INC.
New York   Toronto   London   Auckland   Sydney
Mexico City   New Delhi   Hong Kong   Buenos Aires

Developed by Kirchoff/Wohlberg, Inc., in cooperation with Scholastic Inc.

The Old Man of the Steppe

Long, long ago in ancient China, there was a small village on the great steppe. The steppe was a plain with very few trees. In the village lived a wise old man and his son, Lin. They lived in a small, tidy hut. Behind the hut was a stable made of stone.

The old man was a trainer of horses. He was respected all through the land. He could make even the most obstinate horse obey. The old man had made a fair living with his skill. He was even able to buy a few valuable horses for himself.

One day, the old man told Lin to go to the stable and saddle his new mare. Lin bowed and went quickly to do as his father asked. Lin unlatched the door to the stable and walked into the cool shadows. The new mare was in the first stall. She stomped her hooves, shook her mane, and neighed.

"Hello, there," said Lin. "Today my father shall train you. How do you like that?"

The mare snorted loudly. Lin slipped a rope around her neck and led her outside. Suddenly, she reared up, jerking the rope from Lin's grasp.

"Ho there!" cried Lin.

The mare bolted and ran toward the stone wall. With a graceful leap, she cleared the fence, and raced as fast as she could across the plain.

"Father!" Lin cried. "The mare has run off!"

The old man came out of the hut and stared at the dust rising in the distance. Lin bowed to his father and said, "Father, please forgive my carelessness!"

The villagers heard Lin's shout. They came out of their own huts and joined the old man. They gathered around him, wringing their hands and shaking their heads in distress.

"Oh, my," said one old woman. "That is such a bad, bad thing!"

"A pity!" said a young woman. "Surely fate has frowned on you."

"Ah, no," said a small boy. "What terrible luck!"

But the wise old man simply said, "Perhaps not."

The following morning, Lin and the old man saw the mare returning at a gallop. Behind her was a beautiful, wild stallion. The mare stopped at the stone wall and put her head over. She began eating the hay in the feed box as if nothing had happened.

The villagers heard the commotion. They came over and stood by the old man, clapping their hands and nodding their heads.

"Oh, my," said the old woman. "That is such a very good thing!"

"A joy!" said the young woman. "What wonderful, wonderful luck!"

"Ah, yes," said the small boy. "Fate has smiled on you."

The old man said, "Perhaps not."

Later that day, Lin went to the stable.

"If I train this stallion myself," he said, "my father will be proud of me."

Lin saddled the stallion and climbed on. The stallion immediately tossed him off.

"Father!" Lin cried. "My leg is broken!" The old man and the villagers came out of their huts. They gathered around Lin.

"Such a bad thing!" said the old woman.

"Fate has frowned on you," said the young woman.

"What terrible luck!" said the small boy.

The old man said, "Perhaps not."

The following day, the army arrived at the village. They wanted the young men of the town to join them. A war had broken out.

The captain of the army pounded on the wise old man's door. "Come out!" he commanded.

The old man slowly opened the door.

"You are much too old to serve in our army," said the captain. "But we have heard that you have a strong, young son."

Lin hobbled out on his crutch. The captain stared at the leg, which was splinted and bound.

The wise old man explained, "An incident occurred yesterday. My son was thrown from a stallion."

Lin said, "When I fell from the stallion, I broke my leg. I can only hop."

"Then you are of no use to us," the captain declared angrily. He rode out of the village with his troop.

The villagers came to the hut of the wise old man.

"Oh, my," said the old woman. "You see that what appears good might not be good!"

"Ah, yes," said the young woman. "You see that what appears bad might not be bad."

"You are wise, indeed!" said the small boy. "You see both good and bad for what they are really worth!"

The old man simply smiled.

Fishing for the Moon

Long ago in ancient China, there lived a silly young man named Cho. One evening, he carried his wooden bucket to the well near his home. He was gathering water for his nighttime tea. As he walked along, he sang happy ballads to entertain himself.

Cho lowered the bucket into the deep hollow of the well. As he pulled it out, he saw the reflection of the moon floating on the water.

"Oh, dear!" cried Cho. "What has caused the golden moon to fall from the heavens into my well?"

The answer he got was the humming of the insects in the grass and the howling of the wolves in the hills.

Since he received no answer, Cho answered himself. "I do believe that the rain last night washed the moon right out of the sky. It is my duty to put it back!"

He raced back to his house where he found his fishing gear. He hurried back to the well and lowered the hook into the water.

"Do not fear," he said to the moon. "I shall catch you and return you to your rightful place in the sky!"

He sang cheerfully as he moved the pole back and forth.

Suddenly, the hook snagged on something in the water. Cho, thinking he had caught the moon, pulled and tugged, tugged and pulled.

With a loud crack, the rope broke. Cho fell.

"Oh, my," groaned Cho. "That moon is much heavier than I had expected!"

Then Cho looked up into the sky and saw the bright, golden moon in its proper place.

Cho leapt to his feet, pointing at the sky and bragging, "Look, I've done it! I caught the moon and tossed it back! Insects, you can stop your sad humming! Wolves, you can stop your sorrowful howling! The beautiful moon is back!"

Singing with joy, Cho walked home, proud of the deed he had done.

Two of Everything

Long ago in ancient China, there lived a poor old man and his poor old wife. One day, while digging in his garden, the old man discovered an enormous pot.

"What good luck," he said to himself. "This is a nice, sturdy brass pot. I shall take it to my wife."

The man put his leather purse inside the pot to carry it home. He hurried off.

"What have you there?" the old wife asked, wiping her hands on her apron.

"I found a nice, big pot for our meals," said the old man. "It was in the garden soil and I dug it up with my shovel. Isn't it a wonderful treasure?"

"Treasure?" scowled the old wife. "That old pot? It would be too much work for me to cook a meal large enough to fill it."

Saddened by her harsh words, the old man lugged the pot outside. He would let it catch rainwater. He reached inside the pot and removed his purse. Inside was another leather purse, exactly like his own.

He took out the second purse and opened it. Just like his own, it had five coins inside. The old man grinned and held the coins up to the sun.

As he did, one coin slipped from his fingers and fell inside the brass pot with a click-clank.

The old man reached into the pot for the coin and pulled out two coins.

"Wife!" he called. "Come see this!"

The old wife came out of the house grumbling. When the old man showed her how the pot had made another purse and another coin, she became quite excited.

"What else can we drop inside?" she mused.

"We have one bowl of rice for our dinner," said the old man. "Let's make one more."

The old wife put the bowl of rice inside the pot. Out came two bowls of rice.

The man tossed a basket full of cabbage inside the pot. Suddenly, there were two baskets full.

For many hours, the old man and the old wife entertained themselves by making two of everything. They tossed in their teapot, their mirror, their sleeping mat, their stool, their lantern, and the old wife's slippers. Every time they put one thing in, two would come out.

The old man picked up the family dog and started to drop it into the pot. The old wife shook her head. "Do not put the dog in the pot," she said. "We do not need another mouth to feed!"

The old wife grabbed for the dog, tripped, and fell headlong into the brass pot.

Two old wives crawled out of the brass pot. The old man stared in disbelief.

"What shall we do now?" he cried. "I do not need two wives!" He jumped up and down, enraged. Then he, too, stumbled into the pot. Two old men climbed out.

The four of them—two old men and two old wives—sat down to dinner and shared the rice and cabbage. They chatted about the problem. Soon they had a good solution.

The extra old man married the extra old wife. The two built themselves a pleasant little house next door to the first couple. The two couples lived happily side by side. They had matching teapots, rice bowls, mats, mirrors, and lots and lots of cabbage.